# CONVEX
## AND
# CONCAVE

## The Mystery of the Magical

## Lenses

## Ray DiZazzo

**Granite-Collen**
**Camarillo**

Published by
Granite-Collen Communications
PO Box 621
Camarillo, CA 93011

Library of Congress Cataloging-in-Publication Data


1. **Convex and Concave:  The Mystery of the Magical
Lenses**
ISBN: 0964880059
ISBN-13: 9780964880054

Printed in the United States of America

## Books by Ray DiZazzo

*Washington's Salt*
*The Water Bulls*
*Moonmare*
*The Simian Bridge*
*Corporate Media Production*
*The Clarity Factor*
*Saying the Right Thing*
*Corporate Scriptwriting: A Professional's Guide*
*Corporate Television: A Producer's Handbook*
*The Car Buyer's Art:*
*How to Beat the Salesman at His Own Game*
*(with Darrel Parrish)*
*Songs for a Summer Fly*
*Clovin's Head*

*For Riley, Sidney and Karic.*

# Tales That Teach

**P**arables. Short stories using simple allegories to teach us valuable life lessons. We rarely find them on bookstore shelves these days. In fact, most people would probably regard them as "corny" or "old fashioned" childrens' literature, dating back to the time of Aesop.

I disagree.

Though I *will* concede that modern day parables are not commonplace, it seems to me that simple, engaging tales that teach valuable life lessons should be in demand. In fact, they might just be the best medicine, for both the kids *and* us adults, in these anxious, uncertain times.

On the following pages you will find a story entitled, *Convex and Concave: The Mystery of the Magical Lenses*. I consider it a kind of children's parable with an adult message:

**We can achieve a sense of balance
and peace in our lives simply by being open
to the points of view of others.**

A message with a valuable life lesson? Absolutely. Capable of having a positive impact on us? Of course. But we rarely think about "the points of view of others", right? We're usually too busy and focused on other, *seemingly* more important concerns – our own points of view!

My hope is that this simple little "children's" parable will change that. If I'm right, it will entertain you, open your mind to new possibilities and most of all have that positive impact on your life.

Enjoy!

Ray DiZazzo

# CONVEX
## AND
# CONCAVE

## The Mystery of the Magical

## Lenses

# One

It began on a backyard viewing deck, in the darkness of a cold, very clear night in Rockport, Maine. Sarah and Lauren Nelson would recall in later years that the visitor had come on November 4$^{th}$ at 7:30 P.M., exactly two hours after they had officially turned eleven.

Sarah had spent most of the evening outside on the deck, dancing, singing and blowing cloud breaths into the crisp night air. She would stop occasionally to talk with her dad or point out a new constellation she'd found, then she'd quickly be off again, twirling away in circles under the sparkling blanket of stars.

Lauren, on the other hand, had spent most of the evening inside seated on the couch. With her special function calculator beside her, her math book open and her calendar standing by, she concentrated on homework and planning for her class party on Monday. She'd gone outside only occasionally, zippered deep into her new, green, birthday jacket, with more of a sense of impatience than wonder.

The girls' father, Jim Nelson, kept an eye on both Lauren and Sarah as he went about setting up a telescope and testing it in his backyard. Jim was a telescope maker and an avid astronomy enthusiast. On most clear nights, if he wasn't busy assembling or testing star gazing equipment, he could be found looking upward into the darkness, marveling at a galaxy, a star cluster, or some dazzling new finger of the Milky Way.

On this night Jim hadn't gotten much work done because both girls had spent more time tugging at his sleeve than usual. The reason was simple. They had not received their final birthday presents – something special he had promised earlier that afternoon.

For the third time that evening Lauren stepped out through the sliding glass door onto the squeaky wooden slats and asked the same question, "Dad, how much longer *now*?"

Just at that moment Sarah found the constellation Orion. Before Jim could answer Lauren, Sarah pointed to the sky, jumped up and down and blurted out, "Hey

Laur. Look, it's Orion! He's like Hercules! Look!"

"Yeah, right. Big deal." Lauren said, shaking her head. Then she prompted her father once again. "Dad, I'm *freezing*! When?"

Jim had been expecting to hear from Lauren again. It had been almost fifteen minutes since her last appearance. And he had known that Sarah would remain outside with him all evening. The two girls were identical twins – short brown hair, green eyes, four-feet-one and seventy-one pounds (to the ounce), but they were also opposites in many ways. For Sarah the world was an exciting wonderland. She would frequently stare in amazement at the petal of a rose or run tumbling through a field of tall grass chasing butterflies, or bubble over with excitement at the sight of a humming bird. Her world was unorganized, unscheduled and impromptu. Whenever something wonderful happened, that was the best time, and everything else, rules included, simply had to wait.

Lauren, on the other hand, operated on a strict system of timing and order. Her world was highly organized and logical. If things didn't happen exactly as they had been planned, she was quick to become frustrated and impatient. As for fields and flowers, she might run with her sister and enjoy a romp, but very soon she would end up seated under a nearby tree reading a book or planning her involvement in the next school field trip.

Because of their differences, the twins quibbled often, each one accusing the other of being a "dufus" or "dingbat." While this rivalry had gone on with no real animosity for as long as Jim could remember, lately he'd noticed the arguments had grown more intense. It seemed the girls were actually becoming spiteful and genuinely angry with each other. Names like "dufus" and "dingbat" were turning into "stupid" and "idiot." It was obvious that as the girls grew older they were becoming more and more polarized in their perceptions of the world and the gap between them was widening.

It was because of this, and the fact that Jim knew his daughters so well and loved them so deeply, that he had arranged for the special gifts they would receive this evening – at least that's what he'd thought at first. But over the course of the day he'd experienced some odd feelings that made him begin to wonder if there might not be more to it than that...some strange connection that he couldn't quite...

"*When*, Dad?" Lauren prompted again, breaking his trance.

"Any minute, now," Jim replied. "In fact, I think I hear her car pulling up out front."

"Car?" Lauren asked, hearing a door open out on the street. "Whose car?"

"Dad, I see Orion's sword!" Sarah interjected, having forgotten about the birthday present and caring little about the car that had just pulled up.

"Shut up Sarah! *Whose* car, Dad?" Lauren urged.

"You shut up, pencil-head," Sarah shot back.

"A friend's car," Jim said. "A special friend. She's here now. And you two cut it out!" Then he turned to Sarah, pointed up at Orion's sword and confirmed, "It's those three stars pointing down from his belt. Right there. Is that what you're looking at?"

"Yeah! The three small ones close together."

"Exactly," Jim said. "But remember, I told you the one in the middle isn't really a star. It just looks like one."

"I remember," Sarah said, thinking back, trying to remember what her dad had said about it. "What is it?"

"A cloud of gas, remember? It's called a *nebula*."

"Right!" Sarah squealed. "How cool. A nebula!"

Meanwhile, Lauren had been listening intently to a series of sounds that told her the new friend her father spoke of was approaching. First a car door had closed. Then, after a moment of silence, she heard branches crackling – footsteps on the path beside the driveway leading to the back gate. *How did this person know to come to the backyard?* Again a moment of silence, and then the lock and hinge squeaked. Finally, the gate opened and banged closed, and the stranger's footsteps crunched in the soft mulch along the side of the house.

Lauren looked toward the shadows near the hedge.

Just as Sarah finished marveling at the Orion nebula, she did, too.

The woman stepped around the corner onto the deck.

"Well," she said, looking first at Lauren and then at Sarah, "these must be the birthday girls."

# Two

Jim turned at the sound of the woman's voice. He stepped forward and extended his hand. "Birthday girls is right," he said. "Eleven years old, would you believe!" Then he added, "I see you found the place. No trouble?"

"None at all," the woman said. "Your directions were fine. And I've been in the neighborhood before."

As this welcome exchange went on, both Sarah and Lauren stared up at the new visitor. She was shorter than their dad, and, under a thick down jacket and black turtleneck sweater, she seemed to be very thin. She wore knitted gloves and tennis shoes and corduroy pants. She seemed very nice and she smiled a lot. There was really nothing odd or different about her, both girls thought at the same moment. But then again…

"This is Mrs. Olson," their father said.

But before he could introduce the girls, the woman stopped him with a smile, asking, "Who's Sarah and who's Lauren?" As both girls were about to respond, Mrs. Olson said. "No, wait. I heard some talk about the Orion nebula. Who's the nebula girl?" Sarah smiled, raised her hand and bounced up and down. "Then you must be Sarah."

Sarah nodded and smiled.

"And that makes you Lauren," the woman continued, smiling down.

Lauren, too, nodded, with a bit more reservation than Sarah, and smiled.

"Well, I'll tell you what," Mrs. Olson continued, "you guys may be two different little girls, but it's sure hard to tell you apart."

Sarah and Lauren looked at each other and giggled.

"Who was the first one born? No wait. Let me guess again." She looked at both girls thoughtfully, tapped her lips with her finger, then pointed and said, "Lauren. Something tells me you were first."

"Right," Lauren said with a proud smile.

"And I came three minutes later." Sarah added. "So I guess she's a *little* older than me. But not that much."

"Sure couldn't tell it," Mrs. Olson continued. "You two look like one little girl and a mirror, and which is which I haven't the slightest idea!"

Both girls laughed. They liked this woman. She was happy and funny and it was obvious she liked kids. Besides, she was a friend of their dad's, so she had to be nice. But how come they'd never seen or heard of her before, they both wondered. And even though she looked like just any other friend, something seemed different about her. The girls couldn't put there fingers on it. It was nothing bad, they sensed, but it was... something... It was...

"Mrs. Olson is a new friend of mine," Jim said to the girls. "She's a lens and mirror maker. And from what I've seen, a darn good one. In fact, I'm trying out some of her equipment tonight," he said, gesturing to the telescope behind him.

Though the girls weren't telescope experts, they'd spent enough time around their father's work to know what this meant. The telescopes he made and sold had lenses and mirrors inside them. And those lenses and mirrors made it so you could see the stars up close.

"Yesterday Mrs. Olson and I were talking," Jim continued, "kind of getting to know each other. And she was telling me some things about lenses and mirrors I didn't know. Some pretty amazing stuff...and..."

*Why was their dad hesitating slightly, the girls wondered?*

"…and as she was talking, for some reason I thought of you two. And since your birthday was today, I thought, well, I thought I'd just ask her to come over and visit and tell you some of the same things she told me."

The girls were puzzled by this for two reasons. First, having a friend tell you something wasn't really a birthday present. If it was something neat, like a great story, it might be fun to listen to, but it still wasn't a present. And second, both girls had focused on the slight change in their dad's demeanor as he was talking. He seemed just a little nervous or something, almost a little scared, they thought. No, they both reasoned. Couldn't be…

"But you said a present, Dad," Lauren commented.

"Maybe she brought presents, ninny!" Sarah said.

"Girls!"

Mrs. Olson chuckled and interrupted. "They're right, Jim. It's their birthday and that calls for presents. So I did bring something little for them."

This made the girls feel better. The word "little" wasn't particularly encouraging, but a little present was certainly better than no present. And sometimes little presents were the best. Three years ago Sarah had gotten a tiny little music box that she still adored.

Mrs. Olson reached into her jacket pocket and re-moved a small cloth pouch. As she was doing this she sat down on the deck seat near the telescope. "Come here, girls," she said, patting the cold wood on either side of her.

The girls glanced at their dad, who smiled and nod-ded. Both girls moved to the rail and took seats – Sarah on the left and Lauren on the right. Of course, the girls kept a keen eye on the pouch in Mrs. Olson's hand as they got comfortable.

"You girls pretty lucky?" Mrs. Olson asked, reaching into the pouch.

The girls thought about this. "I guess so," Sarah said.

"Good. And how about you?"

Lauren shrugged. "Sort of," she said, not particularly interested in the question.

"Well, you're about to get a little *more* lucky," Mrs. Olson said as she took something from the pouch that clinked slightly. As she put the pouch back into her pock-et the girls heard the same fragile noise again, like the tinkle of glass pieces. They watched the woman's hand closely as she finally opened her palm. Lying there in the darkness were two circular pieces of glass roughly the size of quarters. At first Lauren thought they were charms, maybe attached to…necklaces? Sarah noticed that they seemed to sparkle more than other glassy things she'd seen, but neither girl had any real idea of what they were.

Then Mrs. Olson held her palm up higher and the cold starlight caught the two items just so. They immediately seemed to light up and sparkle even brighter. Both girls then realized what their gifts were to be.

"Lenses!" Sarah said. "Tiny little lenses!"

"Lenses?" Lauren asked.

"Exactly." Mrs. Olson said. "Lenses. But not just any old lenses."

"Magic ones?" Sarah burst out, jumping off the seat with her eyes suddenly open wide.

"There *aren't* any magic things," Lauren corrected. And she suddenly appeared somewhat disenchanted with this present business for which she had endured a bit too much cold and discomfort. After all, what good were lenses?

"No magic things?" Mrs. Olson asked Lauren. "I'm not too sure about that. What about things like…well, like good luck. Is that magic?"

Lauren thought about this for a second and finally said, "It's just good luck."

"Couldn't it *maybe* be magic," Mrs. Olson asked, "that good things happen to *you* instead of someone else?"

"Yeah!" Sarah said, at first jumping up and down then stopping to think this over.

"No, they just happen," Lauren said. "It's just coincidence."

With a smile on her face Mrs. Olson handed one of the small lenses to Sarah. She had stopped bouncing and was now standing in front of Mrs. Olson and Lauren. "Well, if you learn how to use these," Mrs. Olson said, dropping the second lens into Lauren's hand, "something tells me good things are going to happen to you a little more often."

Both girls looked at their lenses and rubbed them. They were crystal clear and they felt good – glassy and polished. They also felt heavy, which seemed to make them more valuable to the girls. And both girls noticed that they were more sparkly than other lenses they'd seen. They almost seemed to have a kind of glow from inside. And was that a little bit of warmth Lauren felt coming from hers?

"Hey," Sarah said, filled with sudden revelation, "they're different!"

Lauren jumped down from her seat and stood next to Sarah. The two girls placed their palms side by side and compared. Sarah was right. "Yours is kind of…hollow, or something," Lauren said.

"And yours is more…round," Sarah confirmed.

"Convex and concave," the girls' father said.

"What?" Lauren asked.

Mrs. Olson smiled. "Yours," she said to Sarah, "is what we lens makers call concave. It's kind of like a very shallow dish, right?"

Sarah looked at her lens and noticed the smooth indented surfaces on both sides that dipped slightly *into* the body of the glass. It *was* like a small dish… "Or a *bowl*," she exclaimed. "A really small, really shallow one… On both sides!"

"Right," Mrs. Olson said. She then turned to Lauren.

"Mine is kind of…fat," Lauren said.

"*Convex*," Mrs. Olson said. "Yours is the opposite of Sarah's."

Lauren looked down at her lens and realized that Mrs. Olson was right. Hers was just as smooth and polished as Sarah's, but rather than indented surfaces that dipped into the lens, hers appeared slightly swollen in a way. The surfaces formed very slight bulges, protruding outward. "Con…vex?" she asked Mrs. Olson.

"Right."

"And mine is…"

"Concave," Mrs. Olson repeated to Sarah.

For a few moments the girls stood silent, examining their presents. Both continued to notice how smooth and heavy they were and how comfortable they seemed to feel in their palms. And both noticed the very slight warm glow that seemed to come from them.

As this was happening, Jim watched the girls closely. He smiled with love and fondness, noting that their fascination with the lenses was growing just as he'd hoped. With the passing of his wife Claire ten years ago, the girls had become nearly his entire world. "Telescopes and twins," he'd often told friends and relatives. "My two reasons for hanging around this universe!" And now, looking at their beautiful faces and the wonder in their eyes, his love for them and his desire to see them grow up stable and happy grew stronger than ever. Stable, happy …. He turned to Mrs. Olson. She, too, was smiling fondly. Jim stared at her for a long moment, wondering….

The next question came – from Sarah. "Are they *really* magic?"

"Well," Mrs. Olson said, "why don't I tell you how they work and you two can try them out, then decide that for yourselves."

"Yeah!" Sarah said, jumping up and down again.

Lauren kept inspecting her lens looking for some sign of magic, but she found none. Mrs. Olson noticed the little girl shivering slightly. She was obviously uncomfortable and a bit irritated with the cold and darkness. "Tell you what, then," Mrs. Olson said, "Lauren, let's start with you."

# Three

Lauren looked up.

"Okay if you go first?" Mrs. Olson asked.

"Ah...sure," Lauren said. "I guess. What do I do?"

"Well, for starters take that lens out of your palm, polish it in your shirt and then hold it between your fingers."

Lauren did as Mrs. Olson asked, but evidently not as the woman had wished. "No, no," she said. "Don't put your fingers on the *surfaces* of the lens itself, that's the magic part. Hold it with your fingers on the edges. So you can look through it if you want to."

Lauren did as she was asked.

"Now, lift it up. Keep it a little bit away from your eye, and look through it at the stars."

Lauren did so. The first thing she noticed was that the lens seemed to concentrate all the stars spread out in that part of the sky into a smaller area. It looked almost like a "fuzzy ball" of starlight right in the middle of the lens. She pulled the lens away from her eye for a moment and noted that the stars were spread out across the sky again. She placed the lens back in front of her eye and once again they became a starry ball.

"Hey, neat," she said. And just as she spoke these words, she sensed something. Just a quick feeling. A good one. She wasn't quite sure what it was, but it had come and gone…kind of strange…as if….

"See what it does?" Mrs. Olson asked.

"It makes all the stars go into kind of a ball or something."

"Right. You see, because it's convex, it changes the way you see the stars. It gives you a different view. Or what we call a different *perspective*."

"Yeah, they're all kind of…bunched up."

"And that's all?"

"Uh-huh," Lauren said, looking away from the lens at Mrs. Olson but sensing, again, something more… something different. The sensation came quickly again, then vanished. Mrs. Olson was wearing a slight smile. She knew about it *too*. So it really *was* there! Was this the magic she talked about?

"Put the lens back up to your eye and look again."

Lauren did so. And for a few seconds, nothing changed. The stars bunched up into a ball and seemed to glow at the center of the tiny lens just as they had the first time.

"What do you see?" Mrs. Olson asked.

"The same thing."

"Look closely…"

Lauren looked closer at the glow. Still no change. Then suddenly the odd feeling returned and at the same moment she realized what she was seeing might be more than just a starry glow. It seemed to be partly glowing on its own – from *inside* the lens? She thought about this. Inside? No way. It couldn't be. The feeling returned again briefly, then disappeared. She pulled the lens away from her eye to re-check her normal view of the stars. They immediately spread out again across the black sky. They were the same as…. They were…

And that's when it happened!

As if a switch had been thrown in her mind, the odd feeling suddenly flooded in and something marvelous changed in the stars!

In one way they looked the same as they always had to her – like a scattering of tiny lights in the black sky. But in another way, some new incredible way she couldn't explain, they were totally different. They looked…*amazing*! At first she couldn't figure out what had happened. Then something occurred to her. The stars were exactly the same as they always had been. Nothing had changed about them. But now she was *seeing* them differently. Something had changed in *her*. Now she was *feeling* differently about how they looked. And what she was seeing and feeling was so cool!

She drew a deep breath that was almost a gasp. "Oh my gosh!" she whispered.

What had always been just an uninteresting bunch of lights had suddenly transformed into a frigid, sparkling blanket spread across the immense black depths of space. Lauren suddenly wondered what it would be like to travel to the stars…how far away they really were… what they looked like up close…what magic they must possess to be so beautiful and sparkly and full of light.

And something else had changed as well. The cold. Oddly enough, it didn't bother her anymore. Somehow, now that she had discovered the true magic of the stars, the cold only made that magic stronger. The chilly air matched the beauty and crystal clarity of all that was overhead. It was a *part* of the magic.

Then, still another odd thing happened. She began to notice smells…the fresh, wet smell of the dew on the trees and flowers…the cold, redwood smell of the deck planks…the clean canvas of Mrs. Olson's jacket.

She looked up, mystified, and saw her father smiling. She turned to Mrs. Olson. She was smiling as well.

They both seemed to know, to understand…to recognize what Lauren was feeling….how she'd suddenly come wide awake!

Finally Lauren looked at Sarah, who, with her jaw dropped open and her lens in her hand, appeared dumbfounded. And as Lauren looked into her sister's eyes, she suddenly made the final connection – the glow, the funny feeling, the way the stars had changed and even the smells. She was seeing the stars and experiencing the world for the very first time the way her sister had always experienced it!

*The lens had given her Sarah's view of the world!*

"Sarah!" she exclaimed. "Now I get it! Now I see!" And she began to dance and twirl and bounce around like her sister had never seen before.

Still at a loss for words, Sarah stuttered, attempting to respond. Mrs. Olson saw this and said, "A little confusing, Sarah?"

Sarah shrugged, looking back and forth between Mrs. Olson, her dad, and her ecstatic sister.

"I'll tell you what," Mrs. Olson said, "why don't we try out your lens? You do what Lauren just did."

Sarah looked down at her lens. A bit hesitant and "spooked" by her sister's odd behavior, she held it up to the stars and took a look. What she saw was different, but not that big of a deal. The countless stars that were visible with her naked eye had been spread out so in the dish-shaped surface only a few points of light could be seen. But the same odd feeling Lauren had experienced came for just an instant.

Sarah brought the lens back down and looked at it. Then she looked back up at the stars.

"Concave," Mrs. Olson said.

"Uh-huh," Sarah said, still puzzled. "Like a dish."

"Exactly," Mrs. Olson said. "And a concave lens does the *opposite* of what Lauren's does. Instead of focusing the stars all in one place, it kind of spreads them out so you don't see as many, right?"

"Right," Sarah said, still wondering what the big deal was.

"Now take another look."

Sarah brought the lens back up to the sky and looked through it. Blackness. A few tiny stars… But then, a little glow… And the feeling again…

"Keep looking," Mrs. Olson said.

The feeling got stronger…and…

Suddenly she, too, drew a breath as she exclaimed, "What in the *world*?…"

In Sarah's case the surprise was equally strong, but different. It was not exciting at all – at least not at first.

In fact, it was almost a little sad or weird or something. She wasn't quite sure which.

What she suddenly began to see and *feel* was a sky full of stars with*out* magic! For the first time in her life, looking up at the night sky that had always brought feelings of wonder and excitement were just…*boring!* They were nothing but a bunch of lights! Big deal! Had she been wrong all those years? Had she been stupid when she'd thought stars were magic and beautiful? Were they really just…*lights?*

Then, like her sister, she realized something else had changed. She'd suddenly become cold and shivery. She felt as if it were time to get this over with and get back inside the house where it was warm and comfortable… and where her homework was waiting. Hey, homework! That's where the fun and excitement was, anyway. There wasn't that much that was fun and exciting out here after all.

She looked around.

Her father and Mrs. Olson were looking at her.

Then she turned to Lauren, and the final realization fell into place just as it had for her sister.

*The lens had made her experience the world from her sister's perspective!*

For the first time in her life she was seeing the stars through Lauren's eyes! And what she saw and felt wasn't particularly cool – *at first*. But as she thought about it for a few more seconds, it began to make sense. It *was* cold out here. Really cold. And it was uncomfortable. Inside it was toasty warm. There was homework that had to be done by morning – homework that was fun to do and really exciting when you learned amazing things. But what in the world…?

"Get it?" Mrs. Olson said, breaking Sarah's trance.

And on those words, the trance was broken for Lauren as well.

Both girls realized that whatever magic had just come over them had suddenly been swept away, and they were both back to experiencing their own perspectives. After a moment of very odd feelings they both looked up at Mrs. Olson. She was smiling as always. "Get it?" she asked again. "How they work? And how they're going to be your lucky charms?"

Lauren and Sarah looked at each other and shrugged. What they'd experienced certainly had been different and strange, and maybe even magic. But lucky?

Mrs. Olson turned to Jim. He looked at the girls and smiled tenderly. Then he turned back to Mrs. Olson. "They're still a little young," he said.

Mrs. Olson nodded. She thought for a second, looked back at the girls and spoke. "Okay. Now you two listen carefully. You, Sarah, happen to be what I would call a kind of bouncy, bubbly, free-spirited little girl. Am I right?"

Sarah wasn't sure how to answer that question so she simply shrugged again...and bounced a little.

"Take the stars, for instance," Mrs. Olson continued. "To you they're beautiful and magical and they make you feel very excited, like dancing and jumping. Right?"

"Uh-huh," Sarah said hesitantly.

"Right. And that means as you grow up you're going to feel that way about lots of other things in your life, too, because you happen to be quite an impulsive and sensitive little lady."

Sarah nodded, still not quite clear about what she was hearing and what it meant.

"And that's good," Mrs. Olson continued, "very good." She then paused, lifted a finger and as if to emphasis her point, and said, "...*sometimes.*"

"Uh-huh," Sarah said.

"And you, Lauren, you've always thought about the stars a little differently than your sister, right?"

"Yes," Lauren agreed.

"To you the stars are kind of neat, but they're not that magical or exciting or any big deal. In fact, for you, magical things aren't even really true. So you'd rather be busy with stuff that's more important and cool, like the fun of learning new things and making neat plans – stuff like that. Right?"

This seemed accurate to Lauren as she thought about herself. "Uh-huh," she agreed.

"Right. Because you happen to be a little less impulsive or maybe a little less *sensitive* is the word, than Sarah. And that's good…very good," again she emphasized with a finger "…*sometimes.*"

Both Sarah and Lauren were beginning to get an inkling of what all this might mean.

Mrs. Olson helped them along. "And as you both grow up you're going to have lots of experiences – good ones, bad ones, happy ones, sad ones, experiences that will help you, and some that won't be the best for you."

Both girls nodded.

"And some of these experiences are better for you if you're a little *more* sensitive to them, and some are better for you if you're a little *less* sensitive to them. Get it?"

The girls looked at each other.

Again Mrs. Olson turned to Jim. Then she thought again about what she was going to say. "And now that you have these lucky lenses, and you know how they work, you don't have to be just one thing anyone! You can be whatever's *best* for you in each situation… Convex or concave. Two very *different* perspectives, for two *identical* little girls!"

Lauren and Sarah understood – sort of.

But while that sounded neat in a way, it didn't seem like that big of a deal. Both girls looked down at the lenses a bit baffled, but still somewhat mesmerized by the "magic" they had experienced. Lauren held hers back up to the stars to see if it would happen again. The bunch of stars was there, but that was all. The magic didn't happen. Sarah tried and got the same result.

"To make the lenses work from now on," Mrs. Olson said, "you have to think back to what it *felt* like when it did work. That special feeling is the key."

Lauren thought about that – hard. And she tried again, but it wouldn't work. The feeling didn't come back, and nothing changed.

Sarah tried also, but had no luck.

"It's going to take a little practice, but you'll get the hang of it. I promise. And you know what else I promise?"

"What?" both girls said at once.

"I promise that as time goes on you'll both understand what I mean when I say the lenses will bring you luck if you use them. You may not get it right now, but trust me, you will. And luck isn't even the whole story. There's more too it than that…a *lot* more."

As Mrs. Olson said these last few words the odd feeling came back to both girls again – for just a second, but very strong.

*…more to it than that…a lot more.*

As if there was something else…. Yes, there was… But what?…

Sarah and Lauren looked back down at their lenses.

They knew somehow that what Mrs. Olson said was true. They *would* understand. And the lenses would indeed become lucky charms. When, they weren't sure, or how, but both girls knew they would. They felt they had been told the beginning of a story or given the first part of a lesson. It was a good lesson, a valuable one. At least they thought so. And they sensed something else – something about this woman and their dad. A special thing had happened between them. They weren't sure what it was, but they just knew that, too.

What they didn't know was just how much this birthday night and their two sparkly gifts would mean to them in the years that would follow.

That would come later. Much later….

# Four

Sarah and Lauren never saw Mrs. Olson again.

But they both kept their lenses with them constantly, and they began at once trying to make them work. They went out on the deck several nights in a row following Mrs. Olson's visit. They held up the polished, glassy little pieces time and again and tried to repeat the magic…to bring back that feeling… But they just wouldn't work.

Sarah was the first to become disillusioned. On the fourth night she said to her sister, "I thought she really was magic, but these things don't work!"

"She said you have to practice," Lauren reminded her sister. "You're too impatient."

"I am not," Sarah said, and continued unsuccessfully trying to make the lens work.

On that night, and for two more nights, nothing happened. Then later that week their dad was working on a brand new telescope. The girls had been coming and going between the deck and the house as Jim made various adjustments. Suddenly he heard a familiar voice squeal out, "Oh my *Gosh*!"

He looked up from his eye piece and saw Lauren with the lens held up to the stars. She began jumping up and down, twirling and shouting, "I did it! Sarah, I did it! They're beautiful! *I did it!*"

Sarah ran out from the kitchen and began doing the best she could to make her lens work also, but with no luck. "Mrs. Olson was right!" Lauren squealed excitedly. "You have to *feel* it. Remember how you *felt* when the lens worked. Remember what feeling like—"

"Hey!" came a second sudden exclamation, this time from Sarah. "Wow, you're right! You have to *feel* it! Dad, we can do it! We can *do* it!"

Jim smiled, watching the first signs of understanding surface in the girls. These were the first indications that the presents he'd made sure they received would indeed help bring them wonderful lives. And as he watched them marvel at the magic, he thought about Mrs. Olson – the gifts she'd brought, and the way she'd come and gone so quickly. That brought memories of his wife, Claire. . . her beautiful face... her loving smile...

# Five

In the months that followed, the girls began to use their lenses more and more – often in situations they would have never dreamed of. And the results were always good for them.

On one occasion Lauren stayed behind as her fifth grade class began wading through the rocks on a tide pool expedition. She had tested the water a few seconds earlier. It was icy cold on her bare feet. But she could also see that it was crystal clear.

"Come on, Lauren," Jennifer Halmann called to her. "It's really neat!"

On one hand, Lauren wanted to explore the pool and see the starfish and anemone, and the beautiful shells. On the other hand, the water was freezing and fishy stuff was kind of slippery and, well, it wasn't that big of a deal anyway. So maybe it wasn't worth it. As she stood back trying to make up her mind, and watching the others kids move ahead, she felt the small concave lens in her pocket. Suddenly she had a thought. What would Sarah think about the tide pools if she were here? What would she do? No doubt she would wade straight ahead and the cold water wouldn't bother her one bit. Maybe that's what Lauren needed right now, she thought, a little of Sarah's perspective.

To find out, she held up the lens, looked through it at the tide pools in front of her and brought back that same excitable "Sarah feeling" she had now learned to recall whenever she wanted to.

Immediately the tide pools changed. Or rather, she realized her *perception* of them changed. From convex to concave, as Mrs. Olson would say. In her mind the pools became not just a bunch of fishy things in freezing water, but beautiful colors and textures under a crystal clear, wavy sheet.

Lauren inched forward. The greenish gray tentacles of groups of sea anemone waved gently in the water below. They were fascinating, magical, beautiful. And she realized they were amazing, living things. And the cold water was no longer a discomfort, it became an exciting part of the whole experience. Lauren waded forward finding more marvels as she went – starfish with bumpy red arms, small crabs that scuttled into the cracks and crevices when she approached, beautiful rocks of all colors and textures, and zillions of shells mixed in with smooth tiny pebbles.

Soon Lauren had caught up with Jennifer, and the two explored the rest of the pools with amazement, wonder and excitement.

On her way back to school that afternoon, Lauren stared out the bus window at the passing hills and trees, and thought back to what she had done. She realized it was something very special. And, yes, magical. She had used her lens, the magic it contained, to gain her sister's point of view. That was amazing. And as a result, she'd actually changed what might have been a boring, uncomfortable afternoon into an exciting adventure! Even better was the fact that when she'd had enough of Sarah's perspective she'd simply returned to her own way of seeing things and gotten back down to business – like starting to think about the oral report she'd volunteered to give the next day on the tide pool experience.

Although the uniqueness of this little trick had quite an impact on Lauren, she still didn't realize that she'd only *begun* to understand exactly what a powerful gift she had been given. But as the bus approached her school, a few familiar words did echo for just a second in her mind…

*…there's more to the story…a lot more.*

—

Sarah, too, began having similar enlightening experiences.

One involved a field of flowers near Veronica's new house. Sarah had come to New Hampshire to spend the weekend with Veronica, a good friend who had recently moved away. Veronica's house was a huge, beautiful, three story Cape Cod style home with a great big polished wooden porch and three fireplaces. Set in the middle of several acres of trees and meadows, it was surrounded on three sides by fields – one of which was covered with spring flowers. On the fourth side were deep wooded hills crisscrossed by hiking trails.

On the second day of her visit, while Veronica was busy watching TV, Sarah stepped onto the porch and looked out at the field of flowers. They were incredible. Clusters of purple bells…bunches of yellow daisies… even scattered areas of bright red berries. She could also see layers of dandelions and mustard flowers sprinkled out across the field in a carpet of tall, green blades of grass. From a distance it was absolutely beautiful and

Sarah imagined how much fun and how exciting it would be to run out among the flowers, smelling them, looking at the petals, touching them, and picking off several of each – maybe for a bouquet. Then, as she was thinking about this, the butterflies came – legions of them fluttering in on clouds of gold and red wings… touching down on the magical colored carpet before her.

As tempting as all this was, Sarah remembered she'd been told not to go into the field by Veronica's mother, who at this moment was on the other side of the house washing windows. Sarah had been known to have a bit of a problem following orders, simply because she tended to be impulsive and let her excitement get in the way of her common sense. Her dad had scolded her for that on several occasions, and more than one time even grounded her.

She sensed that her problem with following directions was starting to reoccur right then. But even so, her excitement was winning out. What could one quick visit to the field hurt? One run through the flowers? She could grab a few petals, chase a few butterflies and be back in a flash.

She was stepping forward, about to disobey Veronica's mom and break into a run toward the flutter of wings and petals, when suddenly a thought occurred to her. What would Lauren do now? How would she react to all the flowers? No doubt she'd think they were beautiful, but she'd probably temper her excitement with common sense. She'd see the field as neat, but not worth breaking the rules for.

Though Sarah knew this was a point of view she wouldn't be particularly fond of, she thought to herself that it might not hurt to at least try to see it Lauren's way…maybe just for a few seconds before she went and got in trouble again.

She took the lens from her pocket and held it up toward the field. As she did this, she concentrated for a moment and brought back the "Lauren feeling" she'd gotten from the magic in the lens.

Immediately the field lost much of its charm. It was a colorful, flowery field, and certainly it was very pretty. And yes, the butterflies were quite a site, but was it worth disobeying instructions? Was it worth taking a chance by running into a field she knew nothing about? No way! There were plenty of other fields around and since it was now spring, they would all be in bloom. Better to admire them from a distance, then get back in the house and have some *real* fun planning out their next adventure – hiking that afternoon.

And Sarah *did* go back in the house and do exactly that.

She didn't find out until that afternoon on the hike what a good decision she'd made. As they moved along the trail, Veronica's mother said, "Now watch your step, girls, and follow right behind me. There are some hidden crevices on this part of the trail…. There's one."

The three of them stopped, inched forward and looked at a small opening in the ground partially covered by grass and leaves. It was about a foot wide, but Sarah could tell it wasn't shallow. "How deep is it?" she asked Veronica's mom, holding her hand and standing back from the edge.

"Oh, not that deep, maybe four or five feet, but they're also good hiding places for snakes and other animals. In fact, we think the ones near our house are home to a family of foxes, and we've been hearing some talk about bites. I've called to have the field cleared next week."

"Which field?" Sarah asked.

"The one beside our house with all the flowers. Remember? The one I told you two to stay away from? It's full of these. And they're much deeper ones."

Later that evening, sitting on the couch watching Veronica navigate the Internet, it occurred to Sarah that she had done something remarkable that morning. She had used the magic lens to experience her sister's perspective, and that had made her change her mind about something that might have been a disaster. She thought about falling into a crevice with snakes and angry skunks. She shuddered and regained her comfort by rubbing the smooth, polished lens in her pocket.

And, like her sister, Sarah realized that she had indeed been given something quite special, something that could certainly help her be a lucky person if she used it at certain times.

As she continued to rub the lens, the words echoed just for an instant in her mind.

*...there's more to the story...a lot more.*

And she didn't realize that what they really meant would become clear with time...and age...

# Six

The girls learned to use their lenses with great skill and ease as they became teenagers. Both girls had come to realize that they often ran into situations in which their sister's point of view might be a better one than their own. And when this was the case, they had learned to simply take out their lens, remember how it felt to think like their sister, and change their perspective.

Convex and concave. It was as simple as that.

Sarah got into less trouble for being impulsive and Lauren took a little more time away from her planning and scheduling to experience the world around her.

And as these things happened more and more, both girls began to understand a little more about themselves and other people. Sarah began to under-stand what the words "impressionable" and "sensitive" really meant. Having viewed many situations from Lau-ren's perspective, she began to see that although it was good to be more sensitive and impressionable in some cases, in others, relying on her type of personal-ity alone could get her into big trouble. She often re-membered Mrs. Olson saying exactly that when she'd pointed her finger on that chilly night and said, "And that's good – *sometimes.*"

Lauren, of course, realized the same thing – that be-ing organized and more logical was a benefit in lots of cases ("...*sometimes*"), but a more sensitive perspective sometimes stopped things from escaping her that it would have been a shame not to experience.

Convex and concave.

Two different perspectives for two identical little girls.

A way of balancing things that was so simple, but that many of their friends couldn't seem to understand.

Both girls told their friends about the lenses, of course, but found that while they became an interest-ing topic of conversation for a short time, no one else seemed to quite understand how they worked and how the girls had benefited from using them. Also, Sarah and Lauren got the distinct feeling that their friends were more or less humoring them when they heard the twins talk about the amazing things the lenses could do. I mean, come on. Magic? Really?

"I guess it's something you have to experience," Lauren told Sarah one night as the two sat in their room.

"I guess so," Sarah said. "And nobody else can do it. I can't explain it like Mrs. Olson did. Or make it happen for somebody else."

"Me neither."

"But I see them get in trouble because they don't understand it."

"Me, too," Lauren added. "Like Jimmy Thomas. If he'd quit being such a *complete* brain head and have a *little* fun once in a while, he'd be more popular. He could still get his "A's" and have a social life too! Convex and concave. I mean, come on!"

"Right," Sarah said, "And Chad Martin. I keep telling him if he'd stop and think about what he was doing a least *once* in a while, he wouldn't be put on detention so often, and his dad wouldn't keep grounding him. He'd be able to go out more and have fun, but still follow the rules."

Lauren thought about this. "Maybe the lenses are just for us and we should leave it at that."

"Do you think that's what Mrs. Olson meant?" Sarah asked. "Or what she wanted?"

"I don't know," Lauren said, remembering that cold winter night.

Both girls finally agreed that this was probably the case, and even if it wasn't, there seemed to be little they could do about it since no one else could make the lenses work for them – or even cared to try. As time went on, the girls mentioned the lenses less and less. And when they noticed they got fewer snickers and funny looks, this convinced them to just drop the subject all together.

# Seven

One day Lauren made an interesting discovery about her lens. It happened in a situation where she couldn't take the lens out of her pocket when she needed it.

She was seated in her classroom surrounded by her friends. The teacher, Mr. McCall, had begun to read several poems to the class. Before he began, however, he told the class that to appreciate the poetry, to really feel and understand its beauty, they had to allow their minds to open up. They had to *experience* the words, he said, and that meant trying their best to imagine what it might be like to *feel* what the poem was saying.

The moment he said the word "experience" Lauren, who wasn't a fan of poetry by any means, thought of her sister. What would Sarah think about the poetry? How would she experience it? Probably exactly as Mr. McCall had been saying. She'd love it. She'd feel it.... experience it.

On more of a whim than out of any particular need, she placed her fingers on the lens in her pocket, and without thinking much about it, began to imagine how Sarah's perception might *feel* in this situation.

Surprisingly enough, as Mr. McCall began to read, Lauren suddenly began to feel that exciting sensation that signaled Sarah's way of hearing the verse. Without even removing the lens from her pocket or concentrating that much, she had been able to change her perception to fit the situation. As Mr. McCall continued, Lauren began to vividly experience what the poet had written about. The words meant more than just what they said on the paper. They had double meanings and underlying emotions. And the way they were arranged so musically made a wonderful rhythm as she heard them. It was great! She thoroughly enjoyed the class and gained a new, much deeper awareness of the beauty of poetic expression.

Lauren mentioned this to her sister, and soon after Sarah found that she, too, could switch to Lauren's perception without having to actually look through the lens.

In Sarah's case it involved a much less pleasant situation – the death of her pet mouse, Flower, at school. When she'd arrived at class one morning, a group of kids were gathered around his classroom habitat. Sarah knew by the looks on their faces and by the way they began to inch backward as she approached that something was wrong. When she first saw Flower she began to cry hysterically. As silly as it seemed, she'd become very attached to the little mouse. She'd fed him every day, and often cuddled him and let him walk all over her shoulders and her notebook. She'd even talked to him (when her classmates weren't around) about what a mouse's life might be like.

But as her teacher, Mrs. Carson, patted her shoulder and said, "I'm sorry, Sarah. But remember, death is part of life. It's part of the balance of all things. It's okay to feel sad because you've lost Flower, but you also have to step back a little and remember that life goes on for the rest of us – including this class."

The *balance* of things. Convex and concave. It occurred to Sarah then that if she felt sad about Flower, but used Lauren's perspective to help her get back to normal, it might be a better balance. But with her friends all around, taking the lens from her pocket wasn't a good idea.

So, as her sister had said, she just thought about it. And sure enough, it worked. She had experienced the loss of Flower very deeply, but now she was able let go of the sad feelings and move ahead with other things.

Through these and other similar experiences, the girls began to gain not only more of a sense of the power in their little lenses, but also an understanding that they were gaining the power *inside themselves*.

Then, not more than a month after these discoveries, Sarah took the lenses' "magic" even a step farther.

She had gone to the beach with friends and was lying on a towel in the sand. Since she was wearing a bathing suit, her lens was tucked away in her purse behind her.

Karen Toller, one of Sarah's best friends, suddenly leaped up from her towel and said, "Hey! I'm bored. Let's do something crazy. Let's just hop in the cars and drive, and see where we end up at midnight!"

"Are you nuts?" Marion, Sarah's other good friend, asked.

"No, I'm not nuts, Marion. It's been a thoroughly boring week, and I'm in the mood for some excitement. But then you wouldn't understand that…would she Sarah?"

Obviously, Karen was a lot like Sarah. The two had gotten into trouble more than once for making impulsive decisions that later turned out to be quite a bit less glamorous than they'd thought. Karen was one of the friends Sarah had encouraged to try the lens, but who didn't seem to have much interest, or perhaps belief in it. Sarah wasn't sure which.

This time, what Karen was suggesting sounded wonderful. It was different and maybe a little scary, but also adventurous and totally cool. To just drive until the stroke of midnight, wherever it took them… The unknown… Who knew what they might find? It would be like just driving off into some magical novel or love story – exactly the kind of thing she sometimes day-dreamed about.

But then that feeling crept into her mind – that sensible, down to earth Lauren feeling. What would Lauren do now? What would she think of the idea? Sarah knew the answer to that, of course, and as she thought about it something odd happened.

She found that she was changing perspectives without even trying!

The lens was three feet behind her and she hadn't even thought about using it, yet the Lauren perspective was creeping into her consciousness.

Suddenly the trip up the coast sounded a little more "troublesome" and perhaps even dangerous than it might be worth. Sure, it would be glamorous to just take off and drive into the unknown, but what about gas?

They only had a few dollars between them. And how about a map? What if they got a flat in some desolate area? Would they be able to get back home? If not, what would they do? And how worried would her dad be? And what kind of trouble (how many weeks restriction, that is) would she be getting herself in for?

When she had thought it through more logically – Lauren's way – it seemed to have lots of problems Sarah hadn't thought about a few moments earlier. "Not this time," she found herself saying to Jennifer, making sure she sounded extremely casual and cool. "I'm not really in the mood. And besides, I've got some serious shopping to do later this afternoon."

# Eight

It was about this time that both girls began to realize that the lenses were having a much greater impact on their lives than they had ever imagined. More and more they seemed to be faced with situations that might cause them problems if they handled them using their own perspectives. And in every case, switching to their sister's perspective gave them a second choice – an option that usually worked better.

At the same time, both girls understood that their *own* personalities – Sarah's natural impulsiveness and Lauren's more down to earth perception of the world, were still intact, and in many cases *they* worked the best.

The neat part, both girls now knew, was that they had the wonderful gift of being able to use *either* perception whenever they wanted!

Concave and convex.

And the lenses had become less and less important in making that change in perceptions happen. Both girls could now simply focus on feeling like each other, and gain the opposite perspective with ease.

One night the girls sat is Sarah's bedroom and talked about this. "You know," Lauren said, "Mrs. Olson was right. It's a kind of *feeling*. I've learned to feel like you and you like me."

"Convex and concave," Sarah said with a smile.

Lauren took her lens out of her dresser drawer. "Opposites," she said, looking at the lens. "Two different ways of seeing the same thing."

"For two identical little girls!"

"On the *outside*...."

Sarah took her lens from her pocket, looked at it, and thought back to that very cold night. The countless stars...Mrs. Olson's smile...the pouch and lenses...her dad's odd hesitancy when he spoke....

*...there's more too it than that...a lot more.*

"Who was she?" Sarah said, more as a statement than a question.

"I don't know."

"Was it really magic? Was *she* magic? I mean, it was so weird how she gave us these! And how it's all working out!"

Lauren smiled fondly and shrugged. "There's no such thing as magic, Sarah," she said. Then after thinking for a moment she continued, "But…that was about as close as I've ever come to it."

"Okay, just suspend that Lauren way of thinking for a few seconds," Sarah said. "What if she *was*. What if we sat outside one night with…like an angel, or a kindly ghost or something."

Lauren chuckled.

"No, really!" Sarah continued, "Think about it. Think about how she made it happen so easily that first night. I mean, sure we can do it now. We've learned how. But that first night it just happened! Right when she said it would! That sounds pretty magical to me!"

Lauren had to admit her sister had a point. Mrs. Olson had seemed to be able to make the change of perception happen that first time almost on her command. And what had that led to? Just what she'd said. The girls had naturally begun to use their "magic" gifts from then on, and because of the lenses they had slowly learned a kind of wonderful mental skill…an easy change that anyone could do.

But wait, she thought. Anyone? *Could* anyone do it? Not really, she realized. Many people were one way or the other. Convex or concave. And for them it seemed there was no switching over. The convex people had trouble dealing with concave situations...and vice versa...simply because they couldn't switch sides! No, she decided, lots of people could *not* do what she and her sister could do. It had been a gift given specifically to them and it would help them for the rest of their lives....

Just then their father walked through the door. He saw the girls each holding their lenses and smiled, "How goes it, you two? About time for bed?"

"Dad," Sarah said, "who was Mrs. Olson? I mean, really."

Their dad stopped and thought back. He, too, remembered that cold night and the "magic" that had occurred under the stars. But he also remembered the morning before when a stranger named Allyson Olson had stepped into his office with an assortment of lenses, a briefcase and a sales pitch....

When Jim had told her he had no need for her products or services, the stranger had smiled almost as if she'd known that before coming in. "Well, then," she'd said, "mind if I just take a load off for a few minutes and buy a cup of coffee from you? Pretty nippy out there."

Jim had been put at ease at once by the woman's smile and comfortable manner. And the coffee had just finished brewing. "Sure," he said. "Have a seat. And you're in luck. No charge."

The two had begun to talk, first about the weather, and then about business. Twenty minutes later, they were deep into the subjects that were dearest to Jim's heart – telescopes and lenses.

Jim remembered now how amazed he'd been by all the woman seemed to know about the two subjects. She had talked fluently about reflector telescopes that utilized primary and secondary mirrors and lenses. And she was just as knowledgeable about refractor telescopes, the kind that had no mirrors but used an arrangement of lenses. She knew that reflectors were often better for viewing nebulae, star clusters and galaxies because they had more capacity for gathering light – the critical factor in stargazing that most people were unaware of. And she was knowledgeable about lens arrangements, magnification ratios and the benefits of refractor telescopes.

Then he recalled that after they had become very comfortable talking together, Mrs. Olson had changed the direction of the conversation with a comment. "I love the stars and telescopes and microscopes and all, but you know what I've always loved most about my work?"

"What's that?" Jim had asked.

"Changing perceptions. Changing the way people see things."

Jim realized he'd never really thought about lenses in that way. He considered the idea and realized that in a sense it was true. When people looked through lenses they saw things differently. When people looked though his telescopes, they saw the stars and galaxies and planets. They saw the craters on the Moon, and the rings of Saturn, and the moons of Jupiter. And if they used the telescopes during the day they saw birds up close and ships at a great distance and people on sidewalks hundreds of yards away.

"And you know," Mrs. Olson continued, "that's good. Being able to see things from different perspectives is something lots of people can't do. Many people see things one way only."

Jim realized at that point that this woman was no longer talking about telescopes or lenses – a least not in the way he normally thought about them. "How so?" he asked.

Mrs. Olson then pulled out several small lenses from a pouch and placed them on the table. "For instance," she said with a smile, "something tells me you're the kind of man who hates bugs – probably spiders in paricular."

She was absolutely right. Jim hated insects of all kinds, and spiders were his worst nightmare. Their long spindly legs that seemed to feel their way as they went… their tiny fangs…cluster of little eyes…large round bodies, filled with… Ugh! He shuddered for a moment and Mrs. Olson chuckled.

"Guess I picked that one right," she said.

"As a matter of fact you did. I hate bugs, and spiders worst of all. They give me the willies."

Mrs. Olson reached into her jacket and removed a small plastic container half the size of a soda can. She started to screw off the cover as she said, "Well, I happen to be just the opposite. I love insects – *and* arachnids, which is what spiders happen to be, by the way. In fact, spiders are my *favorite* little guys."

Jim knew what was coming. He took a step back. Sure enough, Mrs. Olson reached into the container and brought out a hairy spider the size of a quarter. It stood motionless on the tip of one of her fingers. Then it started to slowly lift and feel with its legs, as if preparing to walk. She tilted her finger over and the spider stepped lightly into the palm of her other hand. There it stood perfectly still.

Jim shuddered again and stepped back even farther. A woman, he thought…a stranger carrying spiders in her coat? "Look, he said, "I'm not sure what your point is but—"

"Tell you what," Mrs. Olson interrupted, "give me just a second here to show you something. And don't worry about little Miss Legs here. She isn't going anywhere. You've got my word."

The woman then picked up one of the lenses and handed it to Jim. "Here," she said, "I figure you for a con-cave kind of guy when it comes to spiders, so here's a convex lens for you. Now, I want you to take a look at this little lady from a different perspective, so to speak… Go ahead."

For some reason Jim took the lens. He didn't stop to think that an eccentric, total stranger was seated in his office holding a large spider that he was petrified of. Mrs. Olson somehow seemed too comfortable and easy-going, and in an odd way trusting, to be a threat – spider or not.

"There you go," she encouraged him again. "Go on… take a look."

Jim stepped up fairly close, but hesitated again.

"She won't hurt you," Mrs. Olson said with an odd smile. "She listens to every word I say, and I just told her to sit still."

Jim held the lens up and looked down at the spider. What he saw didn't surprise him in the least – a hairy thorax…hairy legs…a round, hairy body… A horrible, frightening looking insect face – or arachnid or whatever she'd called it – magnified to even more ghastly proportions. Again he shuddered.

Seeing Jim's discomfort, Mrs. Olson said. "Now, see, you're not letting the lens *work* for you. You're seeing my little spider the same way you always do. Look again. Look carefully at her…."

Jim leaned in and took a second look.

"And let the *lens* give you the perspective."

Nothing changed. But then…

"That's right, let go of how you *usually* feel about spiders."

Still there was no change. Or was there?

"You gotta open up. See her for what she really is…"

And suddenly it happened!

Amazing as it seemed, Jim suddenly saw the spider in a completely different way! Although it looked exactly the same, Jim suddenly realized what an incredible creature he was looking at! The long legs were not really threatening or scary at all. Not if you thought about them in a realistic sense. Actually, they were marvelously graceful and delicately pointed, perfect for traveling over a network of silk tightropes. And speaking of silk, the spider's round body now appeared almost *beautiful* in a strange, spidery sort of way. It was smooth, firm and evenly oval with a light filmy coat of hair. Inside Jim realized were amazing silk glands – internal organs that actually created the fine white threads to be arranged and touched and tucked lightly into place as beautifully patterned webs. And the spider's ability to do that....to move delicately along on the strands of silk, touching each filament into a perfectly geometric pattern. How did it know? How could it sense the spacing? The shape? The exact amount of tension to keep the web taut but not pull the tiny "glued" spots apart?

And suddenly the spider didn't frighten him anymore. In fact, not only was it not frightening, it was beautiful...amazing...a complex and versatile living thing that had earned a place of respect and admiration in the "community" of life. And why? Because of its amazing beauty, adaptability, and the incredible things it could do.

For several minutes he stared, carefully examining each of the spider's delicate and wonderful parts – the face, the fangs, the thorax and each of the slender, neatly hinged legs. Then suddenly the reality of what had just happened surfaced and his trance was broken. He looked up at Mrs. Olson. She was smiling.

It was obvious that she knew exactly what had just taken place.

Jim thought she would say something about the incredible change of perspective he'd just experienced, but instead she glossed it over. "Now, here's the thing," she said. "We all face spiders in our lives – literally and figuratively speaking – and if we only have *one* way of looking at them, well, we're inclined to do the wrong things when we meet up with them. We step on them if they're small or turn and run if they're big. Either way, we don't realize there's no need for either. We don't get the idea that when you look at things in a more open kind of way, they may not even be problems to begin with! And not understanding that, well, that can hurt us – sometimes not much, but sometimes a *whole lot*."

Jim had become mesmerized by the woman's words.

"This spider, for instance. If you saw this little lady any other time, what would you do?"

"Well…I…"

"You'd squash her, right? Step on her and flatten her in her tracks."

Mrs. Olson was absolutely right. Jim stared at her but said nothing.

"But, see, this spider can be a big help to people like you and me. You got any roaches in here?"

"Uh, no," Jim had said. "No."

"Silverfish?"

"No. None that I've seen."

"Any other bugs? Crickets? Earwigs?"

"Actually, no, I don't think so."

"That means you got spiders."

Jim looked around into the corners.

"Get it?" Mrs. Olson asked.

Jim had then began to understand.

This stranger was talking on several levels. In one sense she was talking about points of view – feelings, personal opinions, values – things that have major effects on the decisions we make and thus on the directions our lives take. But in another sense, she was talking about the closed and inflexible way we usually harbor those personal feelings. The way we refuse to change them. The way we automatically persecuted things like spiders…like people?…lifestyles?…races…?"

"It's kind of like convex and concave," she continued. "You're a telescope maker so you know what that means. When you look through a convex lens it makes things look one way. A concave lens does the opposite. Two different ways of seeing the same thing."

It was then that for some reason he couldn't explain, Jim was suddenly struck by a vivid image of his wife, Claire. How he missed her so deeply. How she'd passed from his life so quickly… and painfully…. And how the girls had never known her…. What *was* it?… What?…

—

Just then Lauren tugged at Jim's shirt, breaking his trance. "Dad?" she said.

Jim came back to the present and remembered the question the girls had asked. "Who was Mrs. Olson?" he repeated. "I have no idea. All I know is she came to my shop the day before you girls met her and we talked a lot about…lenses and…perceptions. And by the time she'd finished, I felt she had some ideas that could help you two out as you grew up. And, well, the next day was your birthday, so…"

"Did you ever see her again?" Sarah asked.

"No, I didn't. One visit to my office and one to our house. That was it."

The girls thought back again to the visit on that cold, dark night, and though neither said anything, they both knew in their hearts that magic had indeed occurred.

# Nine

Sarah and Lauren both grew up strong, healthy, intelligent and *very* different.

Sarah became the "creative" one. She went to a respected art school and studied painting and sculpting. She learned quickly that she had a natural talent for shapes and lines. It wasn't long after she graduated that her work began gaining notoriety and respect in the local community, and soon after that she was making a respectable living from her art. As the years rolled on, her wealth and influence grew. By the time she was forty, her paintings and sculptures had become internationally known.

Lauren had great respect for her sister's work, but very little interest in the creative arts. Her passion turned out to be for business. She received her Bachelor's degree in Business Science and went on to earn her Masters degree a few years later. She had gone to work at first for a computer manufacturing company, but she began to explore other areas of the business world seeking her niche. At each firm she worked for she quickly gained a reputation as a woman who was intelligent, hard working, and achievement oriented. She got things done. By the time she was forty she had become the president of a mid-sized telecommunications firm, and a highly respected member of the national business community.

Jim eventually retired and sold his telescope business. For several years he traveled, played golf, stargazed and generally enjoyed the abundance of time he now had on his hands. As the years passed, however, his health began to diminish. After a series of back operations and a period of successful chemotherapy treatments for cancer, he became forgetful and somewhat withdrawn. Not only did it become difficult for him to get around, but also to get things done on his own. This led to a series of regular visits by the girls – mostly Sarah, since she lived close by – and eventually a live-in housekeeper who could keep a close eye on him.

Over the next decade the sisters and their father stayed in close contact. Lauren had previously married a wonderful man, and now had two children. They all moved to Boston to further her career. Sarah did not marry. Instead she had found a life partner and stayed in Rockport, sculpting, painting and helping to care for her father.

And as their lives evolved, both women encountered many experiences in which the "magic" they had learned one birthday night helped keep their lives on a positive and stable course. As these experiences came and went, Sarah and Lauren realized Mrs. Olson had been absolutely right when she'd said, *There's more to it than that...a lot more...* They both understood that what had begun as a mystifying little novelty of being able to switch perspectives had grown into a gift that was truly profound. And it had become second nature to them.

They found that convex and concave meant not only being able to change their *own* perspectives, it also meant being able to openly consider two different perspectives of an idea in general – *any* idea. This helped them to better understand the people and situations they encountered in their lives. And it made them much less likely to jump to conclusions. They both found that when they not only "saw" but also *felt* or *experienced* both sides of an issue, they could always make a better decision about how to deal with it.

And eventually it became clear to them that there was even more to Mrs. Olson's "story" than that! Sarah expressed it uniquely when she began writing a list one day that she made into a kind of picture poem.

| CONVEX | & | CONCAVE |
|---|---|---|
| Hot | & | cold |
| meek | & | bold |
| wet | & | dry |
| ground | & | sky |
| shallow | & | deep |
| flat | & | steep |
| tall | & | short |
| aft | & | port |
| high | & | low |
| fast | & | slow |
| happy | & | sad |
| good | & | bad |
| peace | & | worry |
| wait | & | hurry |

**The meaning of this riddle?     Two ends on a middle.**

### Balancing

*Everything* had two sides. Two ends and a middle – a balancing point. And she and Lauren found that if they remained aware of this idea – if they kept their lives in a kind of simple balance, it lead to peace of mind, happiness, and an amazingly clear understanding of the world and the people around them.

Sarah learned to use this sense of balance to keep her life on a smooth, even keel, while still experiencing the joys of being a highly creative person. She allowed herself to be creative and impulsive as much as was positive for her lifestyle – to do her work and gain great satisfaction from the excitement and elation of the creative process. But she had also become aware that too much of the "creative side" of life was an extreme – one *end* of the balance – it was often unruly and it could be damaging to her.

Lauren arrived at the same kind of balance in her life, but, of course, from a different perspective. Hers had become a world of rapid-fire decision making, highly structured plans and actions, and periods of intense pressure. For Lauren the same kind of excitement that Sarah experienced through artistic endeavors came from managing people and companies... from achieving profits and shareholder confidence and watching growth and productivity take hold in the businesses she managed. She strove to achieve a place of respect in her intense and highly competitive career, and she accomplished her goal. But she found as time passed that when she did not balance her long hours and prolonged periods of intense pressure with doses of "sensitive escape," life became difficult to deal with. And she found, as her sister had, that living her life at one extreme inevitably brought trouble.

Sarah and Lauren thought about Mrs. Olson less and less as the years passed. She always occupied a very special place in their hearts, however, because both women now knew she had given them a very precious gift – the ability to understand and balance their entire lives.

And when they did think about her, it was with a deep sense of wonder and fondness for a stranger who had come and gone as a mystery – a person who had vanished before the truth of who she really was could be solved.

# Ten

I t was on the Lauren's fifty-ninth birthday that the call she had always dreaded came from Sarah. Lauren had known it was just a matter of time, and now time had run out.

Their father was dying. He'd asked for her to come home.

She called her husband, Carl, immediately and told him she had to leave.

"Don't worry about anything here," he said. "I'll take care of the kids and we'll come as soon as we can."

Lauren then made arrangements at work, packed, and boarded a plane that afternoon.

Sarah met her sister at the airport and the two hugged. "The cancer is back," Sarah said, "and this time it's on a rampage. He only has a short time – weeks, maybe even days. He's heavily medicated, but I'm sure he'll know you've come."

—

That night after she had unpacked and seen her sleeping father, Lauren walked out onto the aging wooden deck under a brilliant winter sky. On one side was the permanent telescope stand her father had used so many times to mount, inspect, and test his telescopes. On the other side was the rail she had sat on often and watched him. And overhead, the same crystal blanket of starlight that had hovered over her and her sister years ago as a pair of very similar, but very opposite little girls.

Suddenly she remembered Mrs. Olson, vividly. The thin, smiling, magical woman who had come on a night just like this.

*There's more to it than that...a lot more...*

In Lauren's pocket was the lens – the small, sparkly, lucky charm she'd kept with her constantly ever since that night. She took it out and held it between her fingers. It was still perfectly polished, clear...and warm. Always warm... Always glowing. She held it up to the stars, just as she had done that night. The stars seemed to coalesce and glow in the center of the lens.

This brought a sense of fond remembrance, and again, the question of an unsolved mystery.

*…a lot more…*

The chilly air seemed to be sneaking under her coat, making her uncomfortable. A feeling of anxiety and impatience hovered in her stomach. She focused, remembered Sarah's view of the stars, and of course, they changed before her. The chilly, uncomfortable darkness became a starry wonderland as wide as eternity. The points of light became jewels in the black sky. Angels lived and traveled above her, she was sure….

"Hi," came Sarah's gentle voice from behind her. "Okay?"

Lauren broke her trance. "I'm fine," she said. "How's Dad?"

"He's comfortable…resting. Still have your lens, I see."

"And you?"

Sarah took hers from her pocket and held it up in the night air. "Convex and concave," she said with a smile.

"Two opposite points of view," Lauren added smiling, "…for two identical little girls."

After a moment of silence Sarah spoke. "Who was she, Lauren?"

Lauren looked up at the stars. "I wish I knew," she said.

"And *why*? Why you and I? Do you realize how many people don't understand that simple idea of balance? How many people struggle every day with issues they can't come to terms with, just because they can't let go of their one-sided view of life?"

Lauren nodded. "I know, "she said.

"Was it just luck… or coincidence that our lives became so rich and balanced by what happened that night?" Sarah asked.

"I'm not sure."

"Just something that happened because Dad invited a stranger over?"

Lauren shrugged. "Somehow, I doubt that," she said. "But who knows for sure. Life is such an amazing and wonderful thing. So complex…so simple. The only thing I do know is this. The gift she gave us was very special and, yes, in my mind it was magic. And you know me, I'm not your "magic" kind of person. But I've come to that conclusion. Hers was a magical little trick that ended up guiding my way through all these years."

"Me too," Sarah said. "And you're right…. She was magic."

# Eleven

**L**ater that evening Sarah and Lauren sat at their father's bedside. His medication was wearing off and he became very lucid. He seemed calm and at peace, and he was obviously free of any pain. When he realized that both his daughters had come home, he began to talk quietly.

"Eighty-three years is a long time," he said. "And I've been blessed with a rewarding and satisfying life – in large part thanks to you two. The only thing I regret about all these years is not having been able to share them with your mother."

Sarah and Lauren thought about this. "Us too, Dad," Sarah said. "I wish we could have talked with her and spent time with her…"

"Just known her…" Lauren added.

Jim hesitated. Then he drew a deep breath. "There's…something I've wanted to tell you both," he said quietly.

Lauren and Sarah both tensed.

Jim paused again. "Your mother didn't die from a neurological disease," he said finally. "She died from depression…. She took her own life."

The twins felt the blood drain from their faces. Both women clutched heir lenses and held their breaths.

"She was a wonderful woman," Jim continued. "Creative, like you Sarah…and in lots of ways down to earth and organized like you, Lauren. But she had a demon. And when it came for her, she couldn't fend it off. She tried. She went to doctors, took medications…. She even spent time in hospitals. But she couldn't bring her life into balance."

*Balance…*

"When the depression came she would lay in bed for days. You two were just little bundles then. You'd lay beside her and she'd play with you and love you both, trying so hard to pull herself out of it."

"An….an imbalance?" Lauren found the strength to ask, the tears welling up in her eyes.

Jim nodded.

Sarah looked at her sister. She reached for Lauren's hand. The two held each other tightly.

"I guess I never wanted you two to think about her that way," Jim continued. "I wanted your memories of her to be happy. So I never said anything." He paused and breathed deeply again. "Then, I came across something the other day."

Suddenly, Lauren and Sarah both began to sense an odd familiar feeling.

"There were a few things, a few boxes and close possessions I had stored away. One was her diary."

The sensation grew stronger in Lauren and Sarah. It was warm, comfortable.

Jim took a small leather book with a rubber band around it from beneath his pillow. "I read the last few pages of your mother's diary on the day she left us…your first birthday. Then I put it away and over the years, forgot about it…. But later in our lives something happened…something good. And at the time I felt it had a connection to your mother, but I couldn't *place* it. I couldn't figure out how…" he held the small diary tightly in his hand. Tears came to his eyes "…until I read this again yesterday."

He held out the diary. Sarah took it from his hands.

She carefully removed the rubber band and opened it to where he had placed a bookmark. As the pages became visible, both women read together….

*My dearest Lauren and Sarah,*

*It is a cold, black night covered with stars and silence, yet warmed and glowing with the radiant beauty you two have brought into my life and your father's.*

*As I write this entry your father stands outside on the deck testing another of his telescopes. He is a wonderful man and a loving father. The only thing he adores more than the three of us are his precious instruments and the distant stars they allow him to approach.*

*On the rail of the deck he has laid out a felt cloth on which are a group of polished lenses. For the next few hours, he will insert each lens into his telescope, make adjustments, and view the perspective of the stars each one offers.*

*They sparkle in the darkness. They appear warm, almost as if each holds its own handful of starlight. I feel they give him a power of perception that I can only dream about.*

*Convex and concave. I have learned from your father that in the work of telescope making these are the shapes that create different perspectives.*

*If only I had the ability to use them as your father does. To simply insert a different lens into my soul and change the way I see the stars, the world – if only I could fill my life with wonderful balance and amazing clarity.*

*You are both asleep at my side. Tomorrow you will be one year old. Although I have a closet full of gifts for you, I wish I had the power to give you one more present – a pair of magic lenses. Convex for you, Lauren, and concave for you, Sarah. Two different perspectives for two identical little girls. Crystal keepsakes to help you share each other's souls and find the safest, wisest paths throughout your lives.*

*Ah, to be magic!*

*I love you both so much!*

# Twelve

The next day Jim Nelson died in his daughters' arms.

Sarah felt her father's love and the sadness of his passing with a depth she'd never before experienced. She then used the power she had gained to release the sad feelings and smile once again, imagining the new, exciting journey he'd now begun. Lauren did exactly the same thing…from a different perspective.

Three days later, Sarah and Lauren buried their father beside their mother. And following the funeral, they each went back to their own lives. But they kept their father's house and met at least once each year, on their birthday, to sit together on the deck and share the magic of their lenses.

And amazing as it seems, they found that there was still *more* to the story!

Somehow, with their father's passing and the truth about their mother revealed, they had gained another gift – an ability to *share* the magic of the lenses. Both women began visiting children and adults in schools and homes and hospitals – everywhere they could – teaching them how the lenses' power could help enrich and balance their lives.

"Convex and concave," they would often say. "Two different perspectives for two identical little girls."

**THE END**